Beany
and the Meany

★
  ★   ★   ★
    ★   ★

Beany
and the
Meany

Susan Wojciechowski

illustrated by
Susanna Natti

CANDLEWICK PRESS
CAMBRIDGE, MASSACHUSETTS

Special thanks to:

Neal Dawson-Elli, for the perfect title; Paul, for listening, even when you didn't feel like it; Mary, as always, for your bottomless well of enthusiasm and encouragement; Mary Lee Donovan—without you this book would not exist.

Text copyright © 2005 by Susan Wojciechowski
Illustrations copyright © 2005 by Susanna Natti

First edition 2005

Library of Congress Cataloging-in-Publication Data

Wojciechowski, Susan.
Beany and the meany/ Susan Wojciechowski ;
illustrated by Susanna Natti.—1st ed.
p. cm.
Summary: When Beany's best friend Carol Ann pairs with the new girl
at school to create a science project, Beany must work with Kevin the bully.
ISBN 0-7636-2630-9
[1. Interpersonal relations—Fiction. 2. Science projects—Fiction.
3. Best friends—Fiction. 4. Friendship—Fiction. 5. Bullies—Fiction.
6. Schools—Fiction.] I. Natti, Susanna, ill. II. Title.
PZ7.W8183Bde 2005
[Fic]—dc22   2004051829

2 4 6 8 10 9 7 5 3 1

Printed in the United States of America

This book was typeset in MBembo.
The illustrations were done in ink.

Candlewick Press
2067 Massachusetts Avenue
Cambridge, Massachusetts 02140

visit us at www.candlewick.com

Contents

★ ★ ★
★ ★
★

The Announcement

★ ★ ★
★ ★

It started out being a good day. On the bus ride to school, my best friend, Carol Ann, got the idea that we should spend the next Saturday night camping out in my backyard. I was so excited I kept bouncing up and down in my seat while we talked. We had a lot to plan, so Carol Ann got a sheet of paper from her backpack and started a list.

Things to Bring

sleeping bags	games
pillows	food
pajamas	

Carol Ann stopped writing and said, "Stop bouncing. You're making my writing all jiggly." So I tried to sit still. Carol Ann went on with the list.

Meals

Supper: peanut butter and Marshmallow
   Fluff sandwiches, hot chocolate
Breakfast: cereal bars

"As long as we don't have breakfast-in-a-bag," I said. That's what we had one day last summer when I was at Camp Onondaga for a week. One of the camp activities was to go on a hiking trip and sleep overnight in tents. For breakfast, each of us put two raw eggs, a strip of raw bacon, and a piece of bread in a bag, rolled it up, and put a stick through it. Then we cooked it over a campfire. My bag caught on fire, so I had burned breakfast-in-a-bag. It tasted bad.

Next Carol Ann wrote:

<u>Snacks</u>
gummy bears
cheese curls
red licorice
soda

"You better add carrot sticks," I said, "so my mom won't give us her healthy food talk." Carol Ann added carrot sticks *and* apples, just to be safe.

Then she wrote:

<u>Things to Do</u>
Play I Spy, Uno, Go Fish
Tell scary stories

"I didn't know we were going to have scary stories," I said.

"Well, we are, and mine is the best," said Carol Ann. "It's so scary, you'll want to run into the house and jump in your bed and pull the covers over your head."

"Can you put your camp lantern on the list of things to bring?" I asked.

"Why, are you a scaredy-pants?" Carol Ann asked.

"No," I answered. "I just want to be able to see the Uno cards, that's all." Carol Ann added *camp lantern* to the list and said she'd look for it.

★ ★ ★

When we got to school, Ms. Babbitt was standing at the classroom door. She was my teacher last year, and this year when I walked into my new classroom on the first day of school, there she was. She had moved up to the next grade. I was so happy. I love Ms. Babbitt. She smells nice, and she never yells.

"Good morning, Carol Ann. Good morning, Beany," she said.

My real name isn't Beany. It's Bernice Lorraine Sherwin-Hendricks. But most of the time people call me Beany, except for my mom when she's mad at me. Then she uses my whole name, so I'll know I'm in big trouble.

When I said, "Good morning" back to Ms. Babbitt, I noticed that she was wearing two different earrings. She has all kinds of interesting earrings. She has heart earrings for Valentine's Day, pumpkins for Halloween, candy canes for Christmas. She has snowflakes, flowers, and American flags. She has question marks when there's going to be a test, and school buses for days we go on field trips. That day she was wearing a smiley face in one ear. Smiley face earrings mean there's going to be a surprise or something special. In her other ear was an earring of planet Earth. Earth earrings mean science.

Sure enough, after pledge and news, she told us that there were two interesting things happening that day.

"I'm wearing a smiley face because something very special is going to happen."

"I hope it's not something dumb," grumbled Kevin Gates. Kevin is mean, and I'm a little scared of him. He does things like

unzipping my backpack when I'm in line
for the bus at dismissal. Once when he
did that, all my stuff fell out, and I almost
missed my bus because I had to crawl
around everyone's legs to find my pencil
with the troll at the end. Ms. Babbitt saw,
and the next morning she sent Kevin to the

principal's office. He goes to the principal's office a lot.

"Kevin, did you say something?" Ms. Babbitt asked when he said the thing about being dumb. "I didn't see your hand raised." Then she told us the special news. "Today a new student will be joining our class."

"I hope it's not a girl," mumbled Kevin.

"Kevin, would you please share your comments with all of us?"

"I said, 'I hope it's not a girl.'"

"And why is that, Kevin?"

"Girls are no fun."

"Well, Kevin, I must say that right now you're not being any fun. The new student *is* a girl, Stacy LaRue. I know you'll all make her feel welcome. She's in the principal's office right now."

"Why? Is she in trouble already?" Kevin said, and laughed.

"Kevin Gates, please behave, or you, sir, will be in trouble," Ms. Babbitt said. She looked mad.

I was excited that a new girl would be in our class. I hoped she'd have short hair like me that maybe would stick out, like mine does when I sleep funny. I hoped she'd have freckles. I have lots of freckles—twenty-three to be exact. If Stacy had freckles, I wouldn't be the only one mean Kevin Gates calls *dalmatian*.

Just then, Mr. Shanner, the principal, walked in with Stacy and introduced her. Stacy didn't look scared, the way I would if I was walking into a new classroom. She smiled and said *hi* to the class. She didn't have freckles. She had long brown hair in a ponytail that went way down her back. And she had lots of friendship bracelets tied around one wrist. Once Carol Ann and I

this
week's
spelling
words:
century
decade
eon
epoch
future
past
present
tomorrow
week
yesterday

made friendship bracelets for each other, but mine fell off in one day. I guess I didn't tie it right. When mine fell off, Carol Ann took hers off.

Ms. Babbitt showed Stacy where to sit and gave her all the books she would need. Then she said, "Carol Ann, since you're this week's special helper, I'd like you to be Stacy's guide and official welcoming committee." Carol Ann gave a big smile. I wished I was the special helper that week.

In the afternoon, as soon as we got back from recess, Kevin Gates yelled out, "What's the other earring for?" Ms. Babbitt made him raise his hand and ask again.

Then she said, "Boys and girls, let's go to the reading rug for my science announcement." The reading rug is a blue shaggy rug in the corner of the room where we sit when Ms. Babbitt wants us up close in order to show us stuff or read to us. She sits in a rocking chair and we sit on the rug. When we were settled on the rug, she said, "We're going to have a science fair."

Boomer Fenton's hand shot up. "What's a science fair?" he asked.

"It's an event at which students present science projects, and everyone who comes learns new and interesting science facts," Ms. Babbitt explained. Everyone groaned.

"I should be hearing *yay*s, not groans, because the fair is going to be lots of fun. Each of you will pick a partner and find a science project to do. In two weeks, you'll present your projects. I won't grade them. Two judges will do that. One is Mr. Shanner and the other is Ms. Kowalski, who teaches science at the middle school. Awards will be given for the three best projects. But the grade isn't the important thing. The important thing is that all of you will be learning science."

Carol Ann was sitting cross-legged behind Stacy, braiding Stacy's long ponytail the whole time Ms. Babbitt explained. When Ms. Babbitt stopped talking, Carol Ann raised her hand. "I don't know any projects," she said.

"I have books here to help you," answered Ms. Babbitt. She had a stack of books on her lap. "These books are full of ideas for proving different science facts." She opened one of the books and held it up for us to see. "This page has a project to show that plants need light to grow." She flipped to the next page. "And see, here's a project showing that grass can prevent erosion."

Ms. Babbitt sounded excited, but I wasn't. I hate science. Once we had to learn about the planets, and I didn't study for the planet test because I was away at a wedding for the whole weekend. On Monday Ms. Babbitt told us to name the planets and write two facts about each one. I forgot about Jupiter. After the test Carol Ann said, "How could you forget Jupiter, Beany? It's only the very biggest planet in the whole world."

After she explained about the science fair, Ms. Babbitt told us to pick a partner. "Do it quickly because the bell is about to ring," she said. I got up and was heading toward Carol Ann when I saw her hugging Stacy like she had just picked her and was the happiest person on earth. I looked around at the rest of the kids. Elaine was good at science, so I went toward her, but before I got there, she had picked Linda. I thought of Kathie. She was fun. I headed in her direction, but before I could get to her, I saw that she was arm in arm with Gloria. I looked around.

Everyone had a partner! I almost started to cry.

That's when a day that started out good got very, very, very bad. Ms. Babbitt had us go back to our seats. Then she asked if anyone was without a partner. Slowly I raised my hand. I saw one other hand go up at the front of the room. The hand was at the first desk in the first row, the desk where Kevin

Gates sat so Ms. Babbitt could keep an eye
on him. I quickly put my hand down.
Maybe I could do a project alone or go
threesies with Carol Ann and Stacy. But it
was too late. Ms. Babbitt told Kevin and me
that we would be partners.

"Tomorrow you'll meet with your partners to start planning your projects. Now it's
time to line up for dismissal," said Ms. Babbitt.

I got in line. Kevin came up behind me
and pulled on my backpack strap. It hurt.

Partners

★ ★ ★
★ ★
★

On the bus ride home, Carol Ann, Stacy, and I sat on the long seat at the back of the bus.

"I can't believe you got stuck with Kevin Gates. He is such a meany," Carol Ann said. Just as I was about to tell her how I almost started crying when Ms. Babbitt paired us up, and how I would rather do the project alone than work with Kevin Gates, and how I needed Carol Ann's help to figure out how to get out of working with him, Carol Ann turned to Stacy and asked, "Want to go to the library on Saturday to plan our project?"

Then they talked about how much fun it was going to be. I started to wish Stacy had never come to our school. Now Carol Ann had a fun partner, and I had the worst partner in the whole world. I spent the rest of the ride biting my nails. My mom and dad promised me five dollars if I didn't bite my nails for a month, and I had only three weeks to go, but this was an emergency.

"Mommmm!" I yelled as soon as I walked in the door. "Today was the worst day of my life!" My mother didn't answer. But my big brother, Philip, did.

"What happened?" he said. "Did someone cut in front of you in the lunch line?"

"Where's Mom?" I asked.

"She's down the street visiting Mrs. Kasper," said Philip. "So what's this big, horrible thing that happened?" I told him about the science fair and mean Kevin Gates. Philip didn't even care.

When I heard my mother open the back door, I ran to meet her. "Mom, today was the worst day of my life!" I said. "A new girl came to our class today, and Carol Ann got her for a science fair partner. I got stuck with mean Kevin Gates."

I thought she'd say stuff like *Oh, dear* and *You poor thing* and *I'll write Ms. Babbitt a note to get you a new partner.* But all she said was, "Well, Beany, in life we don't always get what we want. You'll just have to make the best of it. What else happened at school today?"

"Nothing," I said. I went to my room and told my stuffed moose, Jingle Bell, everything that happened. Jingle Bell understood.

The next day I did NOT want to go to

school. I had a stomachache. When I told my mother, she said, "Are you planning to stay home every day till after the science fair?"

"Can I?" I asked.

Mom smiled. She told me to keep her posted on how things were going with Kevin. "Now go get dressed, or you'll miss the bus," she said.

In school that day, I tried not to look at Kevin, not even once. When it was almost the end of the day and Ms. Babbitt still had not made us meet with our partners, I started to think that maybe she'd forgotten all about the science fair. I kept looking at the clock, wishing the hands would move faster. When we got back from Art, there were twenty minutes left till dismissal. I crossed my fingers, wishing three o'clock would come before Ms. Babbitt remem-

bered. Under my desk, I crossed my legs. Just as I was crossing my arms and eyes for extra luck, Ms. Babbitt said, "Beany, do you feel all right?"

Then everyone looked at me, and I had to uncross everything and say, "I'm fine, Ms. Babbitt."

"You better be fine," Kevin called out from his desk. "I don't want to catch anything from you."

When Kevin said that, I think it reminded Ms. Babbitt about the science fair, because she said, "In the little bit of time we have left before the bell rings, I'd like you to spend a few minutes with your science fair partners. Brainstorm about possible projects. Feel free to use the stack of books on my desk to help you."

I groaned. Kevin dragged his chair to my desk and sat down. He looked inside my desk. Then he brushed off the whole top of it.

"Cootie check," he said.

I wanted to say, "There are no cooties here. They're all in your desk." But I just said, "Do you have any project ideas?"

"Yeah, how about if we do something with spiders?"

"Eeeyioou," I said.

"Worms?"

"Yuck."

"Okay, let's do an experiment to find out what boogers are made of."

"You're gross!"

I got up and went to Ms. Babbitt's desk for a book on science projects. Every time I read an idea to Kevin, he called it dumb. By the time Ms. Babbitt told us to go back to our seats, we hadn't decided anything.

I pulled out a sheet of paper and wrote a note to Ms. Babbitt. On the way out of the room, I put it in the little mailbox she keeps on her desk. It said:

Dear Ms. Babbitt,
I do not want Kevin for a partner. He thinks I have cooties. He wants to do a booger project.

Thank you.
Beany

★ ★ ★

On the bus going home, Stacy sat with Carol Ann and me again. As soon as Stacy put her backpack under the seat, she said, "I can't wait for the campout!"

I couldn't believe my ears. Carol Ann had invited Stacy without even asking me if I wanted her to come. After all, the campout was going to be in my yard.

Carol Ann smiled at me and said, "Oh, I forgot to tell you. I invited Stacy."

"My tent's not very big," I said.

"I know, but Stacy and I are going to be together all afternoon at the library, so we may as well just come to your house together afterward. Plus, Beany, I am trying to be the official welcoming committee, like Ms. Babbitt said. And Stacy says she knows tons of scary stories."

"Did you find your big camp lantern?" I asked.

"Not yet. Did you tell your parents to FORBID your brother to bother us?"

My brother can be very annoying. Mom and Dad say to ignore it. But how can I ignore things like when I'm going to bed at night and I'm all snuggled under the covers with Jingle Bell and I put my arm under my pillow, there is a smelly sock under it? Then I have to hold my nose and carry his sock to his room with the tips of my fingers and change my pillowcase.

On Saturday my mom took me to The Great Outdoor Store at the mall to buy a camp lantern. The trip to the mall started out good, but ended up very, very, very bad. The good part was that I found a great lantern. It was so bright that when I looked right into the light by mistake, I saw spots in front of my eyes for a long time.

"This'll work," I said.

Then the trip to the mall got bad. The first bad thing was that I bumped into a rack full of rain ponchos while I was seeing the spots, and I almost poked my eye out. The second bad thing was that as we walked down the mall to the exit, we passed by a store called Pizzazz that sells jewelry and hair decorations. I saw Carol Ann and Stacy in line at Pizzazz waiting to pay for something.

They were laughing. They didn't see me, but I saw them, even with the spots in front of my eyes. If only I had been the special helper that week, I would have been in Pizzazz laughing with Stacy, and someone else would be doing a booger project with Kevin.

That night at the campout, while we were unwrapping our peanut butter and Marshmallow Fluff sandwiches, I tried to sound casual when I asked, "By the way, did you get a lot of work done at the library?"

"We didn't go," said Carol Ann. "Stacy got the best idea. She said that instead of finding a project in a book, we should just go to a science store and buy a kit that has everything you need in it. So my mom took us to the mall."

"We found a great kit," Stacy said as she opened her sandwich and put gummy bears on top of the Marshmallow Fluff. "It's a crystal-growing kit. You just mix some powder in water and crystals grow. It's so easy all we have to do is make a poster and plan what to wear to do our presentation. We're going to dress alike."

"We found the kit so fast, we even had time to look for crystal necklaces to wear to the science fair," said Carol Ann. "It's going

to be so fun!" Then Stacy asked me how my project was going. I told her that Kevin made fun of all my ideas and then suggested all kinds of gross ones.

"Here's what you need to tell him," said Carol Ann. She stood up and folded her arms in front of her. "Kevin Gates, I am going to open a science project book and whatever page I open to is the project we're going to do, and that's final." Carol Ann nodded hard to show that she meant what she said. Her yellow curls bounced. I didn't tell Carol Ann, but I couldn't do that; I would be too scared.

Just then we heard my mom coming with our hot chocolate, so Carol Ann quickly pulled out the bag of carrot sticks.

"Yum, these carrots are so healthy," she said real loud as my mom pulled open the tent flap.

After we ate and played games and crawled into our sleeping bags, Stacy told some scary stories that were not scary at all, but I turned on the lantern anyway.

Then Stacy told us all about herself. She said her family moves a lot. Stacy held up her arm and said, "The day I left my last school, my friends gave me these friendship bracelets, and I promised them I'd wear them forever." When she told us that, I wondered if she and Carol Ann would end up making friendship bracelets for each other. I bet if they did, Stacy wouldn't ruin everything by letting hers fall off.

As Stacy was telling us how she once had to move the day before her birthday, and she never even got to take cupcakes to school, we heard a scratching sound coming from the yard. Then the bushes by the back porch started rustling. Next, we heard a quiet, high

Oooooooh. I slid farther into my sleeping bag.
I thought it was a real live ghost.

"Beat it, Philip," Carol Ann yelled. A
few seconds later, we heard the screen door
to my house bang shut.

After Carol Ann and Stacy had fallen
asleep, I was snuggled in my sleeping bag

with Jingle Bell, thinking about what a good campout it was. But then Kevin Gates popped into my head and ruined everything. My only hope was that Ms. Babbitt had read my note, and on Monday morning she would call me to her desk and say, "I can't believe I was going to have mean Kevin Gates be your partner. What was I thinking? You should go threesies with Carol Ann and Stacy."

I rolled over and hugged Jingle Bell tight.

The Idea

On Monday morning, Ms. Babbitt called me to her desk before school started.

"I read your note, and I thought about it over the weekend," she said. I held my breath. "I realize you're having a hard time being partners with Kevin, but I know you can make it work. So here's what I want you to do. Write me notes to let me know how it's going, and I'll do what I can to help the two of you."

"Okay," I mumbled.

"By the way, Beany, you probably don't know this, but Kevin is very good at science." Ms. Babbitt squeezed my shoulder and smiled at me. I tried to smile back, but my smile didn't work very well.

Later that day, Ms. Babbitt asked if any teams wanted to tell the class about their projects. Right away Carol Ann and Stacy raised their hands. They went to the front of the room smiling.

"We're going to grow crystals for our project," said Stacy. "And we're going to make a chart using some great cardboard we found at Kmart that is bright neon pink."

"It's so awesome!" added Carol Ann.

Stacy went on, "On our chart we're going to use markers that glow in the dark."

"They're so awesome!" added Carol Ann.

"And we're going to have rock music

playing at our display," Stacy said. "Get it? Rock music? Crystals are like rocks. And—"

Ms. Babbitt interrupted them. "What will your experiment prove?"

Carol Ann and Stacy looked at each other.

"Well, we haven't talked about that yet," said Stacy.

"Maybe that should be your next step," said Ms. Babbitt. "Anyone else?"

A few other kids came up to tell about their projects. Ian and Tyler said they were going to make a telephone out of plastic cups and string to show how sound travels. Kathie and Gloria were planning a project where they put food coloring into water and put a flower in it, and the flower turns the color of the water. They said it shows how plants get water and food through their stems.

I tried to scrunch down in my seat so Ms. Babbitt wouldn't call on me.

* ★ *

As we were getting ready for dismissal, I thought about what Mom and Ms. Babbitt said about making the project with Kevin work. I went over to Kevin and said, "When should we meet to plan our project?"

Kevin just shrugged.

"Can you come to my house after school tomorrow?" I asked. "My mom'll drive us to the library."

"Can't," said Kevin.

"How about the next day?"

"Busy."

Ms. Babbitt must have heard us talking, because she came over and said that if we were having trouble finding a time to work together, she would help by calling our parents to figure something out. Right away Kevin said that I could come to his house the next day after school, but not for long.

The next day, I rode on Kevin's bus after school. As everyone was walking out of school to the buses, Carol Ann said to Kevin, "You better be nice to Beany."

"Oh yeah? You and what army's gonna make me?" he answered, and pushed to the front of the line.

When I got on the bus, the only empty seats were at the back. Kevin was sitting in the first seat, but he didn't even save me a place. Whenever the bus stopped, I had to stand up to see if Kevin was one of the kids getting off. At one stop the bus driver called back to me, "Are you leaving or aren't you?" After that I just leaned out into the

aisle every time the bus stopped. I must have missed seeing Kevin get off, though, because the next thing I knew he was on the side-walk. I had to race to the front of the bus, where the door was just closing, and ask the driver to open it for me.

As soon as we walked into Kevin's house, a big dog came racing toward him and put its paws up on his chest. "Hi, Astro," Kevin said, laughing. The dog started to lick his face. He hugged Astro and ran his hands up and down the dog's back.

A voice from the living room yelled out, "Hang up your jacket."

"Is that your mom?" I asked Kevin.

"No, bean-brain. That's my sister, Shawna. Her job is to watch television and boss me around till our mom gets home from work."

I was mad at him for calling me *bean-brain*. I decided I was not going to say another word to him, even though I wanted to tell him how my mom treats me like a baby and makes my brother watch me after school if she's not going to be home.

I was getting kind of hungry, but Kevin didn't offer me a snack, so finally I had to talk to him. I asked if I could have a glass of water. Without saying a word, he got out two glasses and filled them with milk. Then he got a bag of Oreos from the cupboard.

Shawna must have heard the cellophane bag rustling because she yelled, "Three Oreos each, no more. They have to last all week." Kevin took six Oreos and one of the glasses of milk and walked out of the kitchen. I took the other glass and followed him up the stairs and into his bedroom.

I could not believe what I saw!

His room was so great. The ceiling was painted black with glow-in-the-dark stars all over it and model rockets and spaceships hanging from it on wires. The walls were covered with posters of the planets, dinosaurs, and other science stuff. On the floor were all kinds of things made of Legos. I have some Legos, and sometimes I make a robot or a car, but he had whole cities made of Legos, with buildings, houses, cars, bridges, and even parks with everything in them. There was a table piled high with books, and in the corner of the room was a tent. I peeked inside and saw a sleeping bag with a stuffed polar bear lying on top of it. The bear looked like it started out being white, but now it was sort of gray.

"Is that your favorite stuffed animal?" I asked Kevin.

"None of your beeswax," he said, pulling the tent flap closed.

I picked up a trading card from a big

stack on the table. "Keep your hands off my stuff," he said. I didn't see how I could hurt the cards since each one was in a little plastic envelope, but I put the card back.

"You have a lot of trading cards," I said.

"They're from Japan. I collect them. And some are worth a lot of money, so don't get your cooties on them."

Kevin held up a few and let me look without touching them. "This is Dragon Hunter; here's Flower Princess, and this one is my favorite, Keeper of the Keys," he said, holding up the card by a corner, like it was made of gold or something. It showed an old man in a long red robe standing at the door to a castle. He had a chain around his waist. On the chain was a bunch of huge keys. It looked like there were diamonds on each key.

"Keeper of the Keys is the most rare and valuable card in the whole collection," Kevin said. "I had to trade Joe Kelso in fifth grade five cards and three weeks' allowance for it."

"I collect Barbie cards," I said. "But I only have four so far."

As we ate our snack, Kevin said, "Here's the deal about the science fair. I've already got an idea for a project. You can watch, and you can do what I tell you to do, but don't get in my way."

I was glad that we finally had a project, but I didn't like the way he bossed me around. I was scared to tell him he was being bossy, though, so I just mumbled, "Okay."

"It's nothing fancy," said Kevin. "I want to show that heat causes things to expand."

"Oh," I said.

"Here's how it works," said Kevin. "Everything in the world is either a gas, a liquid, or a solid. Like the air in this room is a gas, milk is a liquid, and this chair is a solid thing. Do you understand that part?"

"I guess so."

Kevin went on, "I want to do experiments to show that gases expand, or get bigger, when they're heated, and so do liquids and solids."

"I never see anything get bigger when it's hot," I said.

"It's such a small amount that you don't usually notice it," Kevin said. "That's what'll be so great about these experiments—they'll show the small amount."

"Do you think we'll get extra points for doing so much?" I asked.

"Who cares about points?"

"I do. I need a good grade for this. I forgot Jupiter on the planet test."

"How could you forget Jupiter? It's the biggest planet in our solar system."

"I hate science," I said.

"I love science," said Kevin.

"Why?"

"Because science makes sense."

Just then, Astro came running into the room and stepped right on one of Kevin's Oreos. Kevin didn't even care. The dog

jumped on Kevin and knocked him over, then started to lick his face again. Kevin and I were both laughing when Shawna's voice came up the stairs: "The dog needs to go outside." Kevin took Astro by the collar and led him out of the room.

"Can I come?" I asked.

"I guess you better. If I leave you here, you'll go through all my stuff and touch my trading cards," Kevin answered. I grabbed my jacket and followed him. We walked the dog to the corner. On the way back, I asked if I could hold the leash.

"No," said Kevin. "You're not strong enough. Astro would get away from you, and then you'd have to pay to buy me a new dog. Do you want that to happen?"

I wanted to tell him that I was strong. I wanted to tell him that last week I carried in two gallons of milk from the car, both at one time. But I didn't. Besides, Astro was so big that he probably cost a lot of money. I only had six dollars and fifty cents in my Tootsie Roll bank.

Back at his house, Kevin sat on the backyard steps and threw a tennis ball across the yard, over and over again. Astro brought it back and dropped it at Kevin's feet every time. "Can I throw it?" I asked.

"No," Kevin said. "Why don't you get your own dog?"

"My brother is allergic."

Kevin threw the ball a few more times. Every time the dog brought it back to him, Kevin patted his head and said, "Good job, Astro." I wished Kevin was as nice to me as he was to Astro.

All of a sudden, Kevin said, "You have to go now."

"I have to stay till my mom picks me up," I said.

"Then call her to pick you up."

"She's not home. Why do I have to leave right now?"

"I've got things to do," said Kevin.

"What things?"

"None of your beeswax," he said.

Just as he was checking his watch, Shawna's voice came through the back door: "Kevin, you better peel the potatoes and rinse the beans for supper before Mom gets home."

Kevin looked at me. "Don't you dare tell anyone at school," he said to me.

"Tell them what?"

"That I have to help fix supper."

"What's wrong with that?" I asked. Kevin just shrugged.

We went inside, and Kevin peeled potatoes

and dumped them in a pot of water while I rinsed the beans in a big strainer.

"Kevin," I asked as we worked, "how come you got called to the principal's office last week?"

"None of your beeswax."

We worked without talking for a few minutes, then Kevin said, "I flushed Pop-Tarts down the toilet in the boys' room, and the toilet got plugged."

I almost laughed, but I didn't want Kevin to get mad at me, so I turned the laughing into a cough.

"It's not funny," said Kevin.

"Why did you flush Pop-Tarts down the toilet?"

"I just wanted to see what would happen."

"I guess you found out."

"Yeah, one more trip to the principal's office."

Just then, we heard my mom's car horn. As I got my backpack, Kevin told me we could meet at his house again the next day.

"How did it go?" Mom asked, backing out of the driveway.

"Okay," I said.

"Did the two of you come up with an idea?"

"Sort of," I said, and bit my nails for the rest of the ride home.

The Plan

★ ★ ★
★ ★ ★ ★

The next day on the bus ride to school, Carol Ann asked if Kevin and I had a project yet.

"Kevin's got an idea," I said. "He wants to prove that heat makes things get bigger."

"How are you going to do it?" Stacy asked from across the aisle

"I'm not sure. Kevin doesn't want me to mess it up, so he's going to do most of it himself," I said.

"That stinks!" Stacy yelled, so loud that

kids around us turned to look. "Doesn't that bother you?"

"Kind of, but I'm a little scared of Kevin."

"He's just a big bully. You've got to stand up to him," she said.

Later that day, I wrote Ms. Babbitt another note, like she'd asked me to. I didn't tell her about Kevin doing everything himself. I didn't tell her what Stacy had said. I didn't want to think about that, so I just wrote:

Dear Ms. Babbitt,
I went to Kevin's house. I met Astro.
Kevin is not nice to me, but he is nice
to Astro. I hope he lets me throw
Astro's ball. I met Shawna, but only
her voice. Kevin has a science fair idea.
                                        Beany

* * *

When I got on Kevin's bus after school, he was already sitting down and had his backpack on the seat next to him. As I walked by, he picked it up and let me sit there. We didn't talk the whole ride. I was afraid if I said anything, he might call me *bean-brain* or say *None of your beeswax* in front of the other kids.

At his house, Kevin told me more about his idea. "When things are heated, they expand, or get bigger, because the molecules start dancing around more and take up more space," he explained. "In my experiments, as I heat a gas, a liquid, and a solid, you'll actually see that they're taking up more space as they get hotter."

"So there are really three experiments," I said.

"Duh, yes," said Kevin, and he pulled a big box full of stuff from under his table. "First I'll do an experiment with gas." He took out a plastic soda bottle, took off the cap, and stretched a balloon across the top of the bottle. "This bottle is full of air. Air is a gas. If the bottle is heated," said Kevin, "the air inside will expand, and take up more space. You'll see it because the air will go up into the balloon and blow it up a little bit."

"It's like doing a magic trick," I said.

"Science is not magic," Kevin answered. He sounded mad.

"For the liquid part of the experiment," he went on, "I'll fill a bottle up to the top with colored water and put a cap on it. Then I'll poke a hole in the cap and put a straw through it, so the straw goes into the water. If the bottle of water is heated, the colored water will expand, or get bigger. You'll see it because it'll go up into the straw." This time I didn't say anything about magic, but I was thinking it.

"I'd show you how both experiments work," said Kevin, "but my mom said a grownup has to be around when I plug in this heat lamp. It gets kind of hot." Kevin showed me a lamp with a giant bulb in it.

"Can we call your sister up here to be the grownup?" I asked.

"My sister is busy baby-sitting the television set. If I ask her to come up, she'll just say, 'In your dreams.'"

As Kevin started to put the science stuff back into the box, he said, "The only part I don't have figured out yet is how to show that a solid thing gets bigger as it gets hotter." He went to his desk and flipped through some science books. I sat on the floor and thought about the way Kevin always said *I* instead of *we* when he talked about the science fair project. I didn't like that.

Pretty soon, just like the last time I was there, Astro came running into the room and jumped on Kevin, so we took him for a walk. Afterward we sat on the back porch steps while Kevin threw the tennis ball for Astro to fetch. I didn't ask if I could have a turn throwing it, but after a while Kevin said, "Oh, all right, go ahead and throw the ball." He tossed it to me.

"Yuck," I said. It was sopping wet with Astro's spit. I wanted to drop the ball, but I forced myself to throw it a few times, so Kevin wouldn't think I was afraid of a little dog spit.

After a few minutes, Shawna yelled out the back door, "Kevin, you better do the breakfast dishes before Mom gets home."

Kevin washed and I dried till my mom came to get me.

"How's everything going?" she asked.

"Okay," I said. But deep down I knew that everything was not okay. When I got home, I sat on my bed and held Jingle Bell.

"Jingle Bell," I said, "Stacy is right. It does stink that Kevin doesn't want me to do anything, and Kevin is acting like a big bully." I rubbed Jingle Bell's ear, trying to figure out what to do about it. I leaned back on my pillow and stared at the ceiling. I bit my nails. Then the answer came floating into my head. I jumped out of bed.

"I'm going to think of a way to do the third part of the experiment!" I told Jingle Bell. I think Jingle Bell was a little worried that it might be too hard to do that. But I knew that if I used every single bit of my brain, I'd think of something.

For the rest of the day, I thought about it as hard as I could. I wanted to come up with a really great idea. Then I would surprise

Kevin with it. I would do the whole experiment right in front of him, and he would say, *Good job, Beany,* just like he says to Astro. After supper I sat at my desk and squeezed my eyes shut and scrunched up my face to help me think harder. But by bedtime I didn't have a single idea.

Just as I was going up the stairs to bed after my snack, Mom asked me to latch the screen door on the back porch. "It's supposed to get windy, and I don't want that door banging all night." I went out and latched the door by putting the hook that's screwed into the screen door into the round metal circle that's screwed into the door frame. Then I let out a scream. Mom, Dad, and Philip came running.

"What's wrong?" Dad asked.

"Nothing," I said, jumping up and down. "I just figured out how to do the last part of the science experiment. We need to heat something and prove that it gets bigger when it's hot. What if we heated up this hook, and then it wouldn't fit into the circle part anymore?" I clapped my hands.

"Hold on," said Dad. "First of all, let's call these pieces of hardware by their right names. They're called a hook and eye. Now, let's see." He lowered the hook into the eye, lifted it out, then put it back in. "You have a great idea," he said, "but the hook is so small that even if you heat it, it'll still fit into the eye. You'll need something bigger than the hook; something that will barely fit through the eye before it's heated." We went to the basement, and I started poking through Dad's workbench drawers.

"Don't help me," I said. "I want to figure it out myself." In one of the drawers, I found another eye, just like the one on the screen door. Then I found a nail that had a big top on it. The top of the nail barely fit through the eye. "Maybe this will work," I said.

"I think it will," said Dad. He pounded the nail into the end of a long, skinny piece of wood, so we'd have a handle to hold on to when we heated the nail. Then Dad helped me heat the nail over the stove. "Don't ever do this without a grownup," he said.

I held my breath as I tried to put the top of the hot nail through the eye. It wouldn't fit through! I started *yay*ing and clapping and jumping up and down.

Mom said, "My little scientist."

Dad said, "Future Nobel Prize winner."

Philip didn't say anything. His mouth was full of Cheerios.

The next morning before school, Kevin came to my desk and asked when I could come to his house again to work on the project. I wanted to tell Kevin my idea right then, but I didn't. I knew it would be more fun to wait and surprise him the next time we got together.

"Why don't you come to my house?" I asked. "My mom is home, so she can be the grownup to watch us use the heat lamp."

"Can't," said Kevin.

"Why not?"

"None of your beeswax."

"But the science fair is in a few days. We have to get everything done."

"Look, nosy, the reason I can't come is that my mom can't pick me up from your house. She doesn't get home from work till five-thirty."

"Well, how about if you come over after supper?"

"She has another job she goes to at night."

"Can your dad drive you?"

Kevin crossed his arms in front of his chest. "No."

"How come?"

"None of your beeswax, dalmatian," Kevin said. Then he walked away.

When I got home from school, I asked my mom if she'd drive Kevin back to his house if he could come over the next day.

"Sure, sweetie," she said.

I was nervous calling Kevin on the phone, but I was so excited to have him see my idea that I forced myself to do it. I wrote what I would say on a piece of paper, took a deep breath, then dialed. As soon as Kevin answered, I quickly read: "Hi, Kevin. This is Beany. If you come over to my house on the bus tomorrow, my mom will drive you

home. Bring your box of science stuff to school. Bye." The only problem was that I forgot to wait for Kevin's answer. I hung up as soon as I finished reading.

"Did you talk to Kevin about coming over tomorrow?" my mom asked, when she came upstairs at bedtime to read to me.

"Yeah," I answered.

"Is he coming?"

"He might."

Kevin showed up at school the next morning carrying the big box of science stuff. His backpack was on top of it. He dumped everything on his desk and said, "Whew." Then he came over to my desk and asked why I had hung up on him.

At my house after school, Mom and I sat at the kitchen table and watched as Kevin heated the soda bottle with the balloon on top. Just like Kevin had told me, the balloon got a little bigger.

"Whatever you do, don't tell him it's like magic," I whispered to my mom.

Next, he filled a plastic bottle with water and asked me what color I wanted the water to be.

"Red," I said. So Kevin put a few drops of red food coloring, the kind we use to color frosting, into the water. Then he screwed the cap onto the bottle. He had already punched a hole in it. Next he put a straw into the hole in the cap and put Silly Putty around it, so that it wouldn't leak when the water came up. As he was heating the bottle, Philip came home, so he watched, too.

"I picked the color for the water," I told Philip.

When Kevin heated the bottle, red water came up into the straw.

"Cool," said Philip.

"Kevin, what wonderful experiments," said my mom.

"My only problem is thinking of an experiment to show that a solid expands," Kevin told my family.

When he said that, I went to the counter and brought the nail and the eye to the

table. "Kevin," I said, "I have a surprise. I thought of a third experiment."

"You what?" Kevin asked.

I didn't answer. I just did the experiment. When the heated nail wouldn't fit through the eye, Kevin said, "You thought of this?"

"All by myself," I said, smiling.

"She really did," added Philip.

Kevin didn't say, *Good job, Beany.* He walked up to me and gave me a high-five, and that was even better. We celebrated with brownies and milk. Then my mom drove Kevin home.

The next week, we met three more times to practice the experiments, rehearse our talk to the judges, and write a report about our project. Carol Ann and Stacy told me they were busy working on their project, too, but it seemed like they were mostly shopping at the mall for matching outfits.

"Should we have music?" I asked Kevin at one of our last meetings. "My brother has lots of CDs I could pick from."

"No music. This is a science project, not a rock show."

"What about posters?" I suggested. "I could make some really great posters with paint that has glitter in it. Carol Ann and Stacy found the paint in a craft store and said we could use some."

"Posters would be okay, but don't use glitter. Remember, we're not putting on a show," said Kevin.

The next day, I wrote a note to Ms. Babbitt.

Dear Ms. Babbitt,
I am helping with the experiment because of my screen door. And I am making posters. They do NOT have glitter paint. They do NOT glow in the dark.
　　Kevin lets me throw the ball to Astro. When I do it, I don't say yuck, but I am thinking it.
Beany

Two days before the science fair, Ms. Babbitt had a meeting with each of the teams. When she met with Kevin and me, she said, "Your project is wonderful. I'm proud of you."

That day after school, Kevin and I did a dress rehearsal; that's when you pretend it's the real thing. We set up everything just the way we would for the real fair. My mom, dad, Philip, and Jingle Bell pretended they

were the judges. When we were about to start, Kevin told me I would have to say some of the speech we had written.

"I can't. You have to do it. Please, pretty please, pretty please with gummy bears on top?" I begged. Kevin shook his head no.

"I'll give you my best Barbie trading card." Kevin laughed and handed me the speech. He had circled the parts I should say.

"You can do it, Beany," he said. And I did.

When we finished the presentation, everyone clapped.

Philip stood up, grabbed a spoon from the table, and held it up like it was a microphone. "And the first–prize winners are . . ." he said. Then he beat on the table like it was a drum. "Beany and Kevin!"

"C'mon, Philip, get real," I said. "There's no way we're going to win first prize. The most I'm hoping for is third."

Kevin said, "Winning doesn't matter." But he was smiling when he said it, so I thought that maybe it did matter, just a little bit.

The next day, I wrote Ms. Babbitt a note. It said:

Dear Ms. Babbitt,
Yesterday Kevin called me Beany and not bean-brain.

Beany

The Experiments

Heat makes things get bigger:

A. Gas

B. Liquid

C. Solid

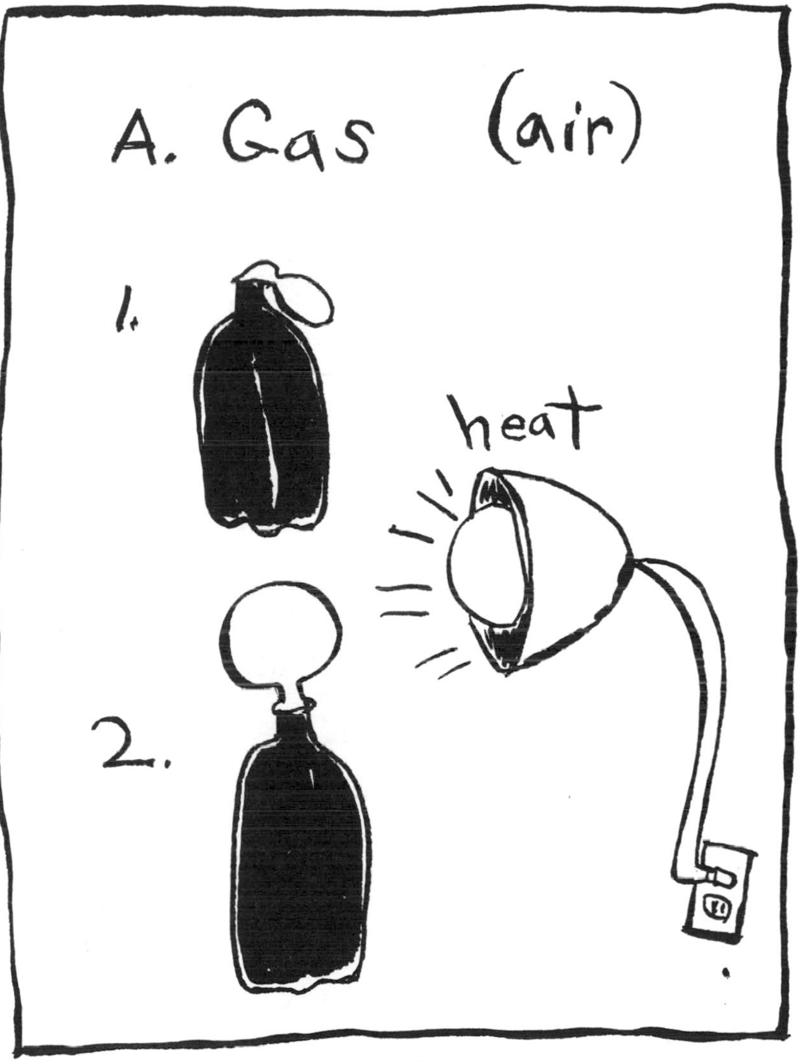
A. Gas (air)
1.
heat
2.

B. Liquid

1.

2.

heat

C. Solid

1.

2.

heat

The Science Fair

★ ★ ★
 ★   ★

On the day of the science fair, I woke up early, before the alarm went off. I lay in bed hugging Jingle Bell and worrying.

"What if our project is the worst one there?" I said to Jingle Bell. "What if I mess up when I do my part for the judges? What if the judges laugh when they walk away from our table? What if Ms. Babbitt told us that she liked our project just to be nice?" Ms. Babbitt would do something like that. Once I heard my dad tell my mom that

Ms. Babbitt does a good job of building self-esteem. When I asked him what that meant, he said she works hard to make us kids feel good about ourselves.

Jingle Bell understood that there was a lot to worry about.

On the bus that morning, I saw that Carol Ann and Stacy were dressed alike. They wore jeans and T-shirts that said *Crystals Rock* on the front. They wore crystal necklaces.

Carol Ann and Stacy didn't seem worried. They were talking nonstop about how much fun the science fair was going to be.

"We're handing out rock candy to everyone who comes to see our project," Carol Ann said. "I bet we win first prize."

"Well, maybe second," said Stacy. "The volcano project sounds really great."

Nathaniel and Montrell's project was about how volcanoes erupt. They were

going to build a volcano out of papier-mâché and put something inside that would make it get all bubbly, like a volcano erupting.

Stacy said to me, "Your project is good, too," but I knew she was just doing self-esteem on me.

After lunch we went into the gym. There were three rows of tables with four tables in each row set up at one end of the gym.

"You have a half-hour to set up your projects," Ms. Babbitt said. "And have fun," she added. I felt like throwing up.

Kevin and I covered our table with a white tablecloth that my mom let us use. It had a big gravy stain in the middle, but she said we could set something on top of the stain so it wouldn't show. We laid out our stuff and a sign. I taped my posters to the front of the table.

Gases, liquids, and solids get bigger when they're heated up. It is Not Magic! It is Science!

When we were finished setting up, I walked around the gym to see what the other teams were doing. When I saw the volcano, I ran back to our table. "Kevin, you should see the volcano. It's huge. Why didn't we think of a volcano?"

Before Kevin could say anything, I ran off to look at other projects, then went back to report to Kevin. "Carol Ann and Stacy have streamers all around the edge of their table. Why didn't we think of that? Should I call my mom to ask if she'll run out and buy us some streamers? She'd do it. I know she would."

"We don't need streamers," said Kevin.

I left our table again, then went back with more news. "Manuel and Boomer are doing a planet project, and they have a black tablecloth with stars all over it. Why didn't we use a cool tablecloth instead of a dumb white one with a gravy stain on it?"

"You need to chill," said Kevin. "Forget about what other people are doing and just—" But before Kevin could finish, I ran off again. In a minute I was back.

"Linda and Elaine have bubbles for their project, big ones!" I said, out of breath. "Everybody loves bubbles. Why didn't we do bubbles?"

"Beany," he said, "could you go get some paper towels in case the red water comes up to the top of the straw and runs over?"

Then I noticed the crowd of kids around the table next to ours. I peeked over. It was Shaleeta and Jessica's project. They had a bunch of big balloons on their table and a plate sprinkled with black pepper. "Oh no," I said to Kevin. "Look at all those balloons! Balloons are even better than bubbles! How come we only have one itsy bitsy one in our project?"

Shaleeta rubbed a balloon on her arm and then held the balloon a few inches above the plate of pepper. The pepper jumped right off the plate onto the balloon.

"That happens because of static electricity," Shaleeta explained. Everyone said, "Wow." One kid even said, "That's a winner."

My stomach started to hurt. I told Kevin I had to go to Mrs. Facinelli's office to lie down. Mrs. Facinelli is the school nurse. She has *Ranger Rick* magazines we can look at while we try to feel better.

"If I'm not back by the time it's our turn, you go ahead without me," I said. I almost got away, but Kevin grabbed my arm.

"Paper towels," he said.

Parents started to come into the gym and walk from table to table. Teachers from our school brought their classes to see the projects, too. When I saw my mom and dad, I waved to them, and they came over to wish us luck. Kevin said his mom was going to try to get off work early and come, but even though he kept looking toward the door and looking all around the gym, I don't think he saw her.

Then the judges showed up and went from table to table. I started to bite my nails. When they got to the balloon table, I knew we were next. My knees got wobbly.

As the judges walked to our table, Kevin took one last look toward the gym door. He started waving. "She made it," he said. I looked toward the door and saw a woman coming into the gym. She looked out of breath, like she'd been running.

Mr. Shanner said, "Hi, Beany and Kevin. What do we have here?"

"We have a project to show that heat makes things expand, or get bigger," Kevin said.

Then he poked me with his elbow, and I said, "We will now show how heat makes gases expand." Then Kevin did the experiment with the balloon on the bottle and explained everything he was doing as he went along.

Next I said, "We will now show how heat makes liquids expand." Kevin did the bottle and straw experiment and explained it. We did not need paper towels. The red water didn't come up too high, just high enough.

Then it was Kevin's turn to talk. He said,

"We will now show how heat makes solids expand." This time I did the experiment, the one with the nail and the eye. When we were finished, Mr. Shanner said, "Hmm." The judges wrote stuff on clipboards and asked us a few questions. They shook our hands and moved on to the next table.

"Why weren't they smiling when they shook our hands?" I asked Kevin. "Why didn't they say *wow* when the water came up the straw? Why did Mr. Shanner say *hmm*? What were they writing on their clipboards?"

Kevin sat down and smiled. "We did a good job," he said.

While we were waiting for the judges to make their decisions, I went over to Carol Ann and Stacy's table and asked how their presentation went.

"Well," said Carol Ann, "I think the

judges liked our outfits and the necklaces, but they told us to turn off the music so they could hear us better. Plus, we were supposed to start growing the crystals a few days ago, only we forgot to read the instructions on the box. We didn't do it till this morning, so the crystals are kind of small."

I looked at the fish bowl of water on their table. It had a string going through the water and the crystals were supposed to be growing on the string, but all I could see was a little bit of pink grainy stuff on one part of the string.

"And," Stacy added, "Boomer's mom broke a tooth eating our rock candy."

"How did yours go?" Carol Ann asked me.

"Okay, I guess."

The judges came back into the gym. We all went back to our tables. I crossed my fingers. Ms. Kowalski said, "We were very impressed with the efforts of all the students. We hope they are as proud of themselves as we are of them."

Then Mr. Shanner said, "It was hard for us to choose the three best, but after much deliberation, we have chosen for third place the static electricity experiment. It was creative and educational." Shaleeta and Jessica screamed.

My only hope had been third place. I sighed. I uncrossed my fingers and clapped as they went up to get their certificates and third-place ribbons.

Next, Ms. Kowalski gave the second-place award. It went to the volcano project. "Nathaniel and Montrell's volcano was impressive," she said, "but it was their charts and their explanation of what causes a volcano to erupt that we especially liked. Those were thorough and easy to understand."

After the clapping, Mr. Shanner coughed, then said, "Now, for the first-place project. We felt the winning project was a fine example of real science. It was organized, clear, and complete."

I knew we wouldn't get first place. I started reciting the sevens times tables in my head, just to keep myself from crying. But right at seven times four, Kevin started pushing me out from behind our table.

"Go," he said. "We won."

"We what?"

"We won."

I screamed and jumped up and down. I couldn't believe it!

Kevin and I each got a certificate and a blue ribbon that had FIRST PLACE, SCIENCE FAIR stamped on it in gold letters. Ms. Babbitt hugged us. Then she whispered in my ear, "I knew you could

make it work." My mom and dad came up and hugged us. So did Kevin's mom.

"Thanks for coming," I heard Kevin say to her.

"I wouldn't have missed it for anything. I'm just sorry I was late," she said. Then his mom pulled a camera out of her purse. "Say *cheeseburger*," she told Kevin and me.

"Aw, Mom, come on," Kevin said. But he smiled.

After the kids in our class were finished telling us *Great job* and *Good work* and *I knew you would win,* Kevin and I cleared off our table. Our parents helped.

"We need to celebrate," my dad said as he and Kevin's mom folded the tablecloth. "Can I interest anyone in going out for ice cream?" We were all interested.

I got a cone-head sundae with chocolate

ice cream and Reese's Pieces on it. As I was trying to scrape the last Reese's Piece onto my spoon, I said to Kevin, "I have to tell you something, I wrote Ms. Babbitt a note that I didn't want you for a partner. I'm sorry."

Kevin shrugged and said, "That's okay. I did the same thing."

The next day was a very, very good day. First, on the bus going to school, Carol Ann got a great idea. She said that Stacy and I should come to her house for a sleepover the next weekend and watch videos and eat popcorn and stay up all night.

"And we can make friendship bracelets for each other, too," added Stacy. "I know you two are best friends, but can I be second best friend to both of you?"

"If you have room for another bracelet," I said.

When we got to school, another good thing happened. On my desk was a small box wrapped in white tissue paper. I looked around the room trying to figure out who had put it there. Then I sat down and carefully took off the tissue. Inside the box was a trading card in a plastic envelope. It was Keeper of the Keys.

I looked over at Kevin. He didn't see me; he was busy rummaging through his desk for something. But I smiled at him anyway.

Keeper of the Keys